D0468213

ALLIGATOR SUE

You mean to tell me you never heard of Alligator Sue, who was half Gator and half Girl? They say the Girl came from her mama and her daddy, and the Alligator . . . well, that's a story you just got to hear.

BY SHARON ARMS DOUCET
PICTURES BY ANNE WILSDORF

MELANIE KROUPA BOOKS
FARRAR, STRAUS AND GIROUX • NEW YORK

For the one and only Melissa Louise,
who knows how to make things happen
—S.A.D.
For Harriett, the Princess of New Zealand,
and my sweet friend Jill, with all my love
—A.W.

AUTHOR'S NOTE

Alligator Sue's story takes place not so long ago in the great Atchafalaya Basin of southern Louisiana. "Atchafalaya" (pronounced uh-chah-fuh-LIE-ya) is an Atta-kapas Indian word meaning "long river." America's largest river-basin swamp, it is 120 miles long and covers 1.4 million acres filled with cypress trees, alligators, snakes, beavers, muskrats, fish, crawfish, birds, and even bears and panthers. "Swampers" like Sue's family live in or near the basin and make their living fishing and trapping. Most of them are Cajuns, descendants of French exiles from Canada known for their French language and music, their spicy food, and their love of life.

Text copyright © 2003 by Sharon Arms Doucet
Illustrations copyright © 2003 by Anne Wilsdorf
All rights reserved
Distributed in Canada by Douglas & McIntyre Ltd.
Color separations by Chroma Graphics PTE Ltd.
Printed and bound in the United States of America by Berryville Graphics
Designed by Jennifer Browne
First edition, 2003
3   5   7   9   10   8   6   4   2

Library of Congress Cataloging-in-Publication Data
Doucet, Sharon Arms.
    Alligator Sue / by Sharon Arms Doucet ; pictures by Anne Wilsdorf.— 1st ed.
        p.   cm.
    Summary: After being separated from her parents by a hurricane on the bayou, a young
girl is raised by an alligator and later must discover who she really is.
    ISBN 0-374-30218-9
    [1. Alligators—Fiction.   2. Identity—Fiction.   3. Tall tales.]   I. Wilsdorf, Anne, ill.   II.
Title.

PZ7.D7442 Al 2003
[E]—dc21

2001029385

PART ONE

ALLiGAToR

Once upon a long-ago time, on a houseboat deep in Louisiana's Atchafalaya Swamp, lived an ordinary Girl named Suzanne Marie Sabine Chicot Thibodeaux. Her mama and daddy called her Sue for short.

One lazy summer afternoon, the Atchafalaya air grew heavier than a catfish's bath towel, and hot enough to melt the wax in your ears. At the cookstove, Sue's mama stirred a muskrat gumbo. Her daddy was playing Sue's favorite double-time tune on his accordion and crooning in a voice as rich as pecan pralines.

And Sue, she was two-stepping and toe-tapping around the deck of the houseboat, singing at the top of her rackety voice, *"O yé yaie, mon coeur fait mal"* (French for "Oh dear, my heart is aching"). You see, every one of her daddy's Cajun songs had to do with a broken heart.

When the last accordion note finished quivering through the swamp, Sue's daddy held up a finger and sniffed. "Pressure's dropping," he said. "Storm's coming, I guarantee."

At that very moment a Hurricane reached down its gusty fingers and whooshed Sue high into the angry sky. Before she could say *O yé yaie*, she was spinning higher than the tallest cypress tree, with the houseboat disappearing far below.

Sue tossed and tumbled as the storm seethed and swirled.
At last it dropped her like a hot *patate*, right into the arms of
an ancient live oak tree. There, croaking out her favorite song
for courage, Sue curled up and shivered through that long and
stormy night.

When morning peeked in on her, the Hurricane was long gone, and the sun rose hotter than a cayenne pepper. Eyeing the sweet marsh grass far below, Sue took a deep breath, closed her eyes, and made a jump for it.

When her eyeballs popped open, Sue's heart nearly stopped. There she was in a Gator nest, nose to snout with a queen-size, prickly backed, saw-toothed mama Alligator.

Sue's knees started knocking and her teeth started clacking. The Alligator advanced. Sue crawfished. The Gator shuffled forward.

This swampy tango went on until Sue could feel that reptile's fishy breath on her cheek. "Aw," said Sue finally, "go on and eat me." And she fainted dead away.

That mama Gator snuffled up to Sue. "Poor puny li'l thing," she crooned, tucking some Spanish moss over her. And with a crooked grin, she set to singing Sue an Alligator lullaby.

From that day on, Mama Coco adopted Sue as one of her own. When the nestful of eggs had busted open and all the bulgy-eyed stripedy little Gators had wriggled out, Sue found herself in a foster family with seventeen brothers and thirteen sisters.

Before long her daddy's song faded in the back room of her memory, and Sue forgot to remember the days when she'd been a Girl. "Home" came to mean a cozy den in the ancient mud of the great swamp and the comforting grunts of the Alligator clan.

Mama Coco set to teaching her children the ways of the Alligator. Sue learned to waddle on all fours and to talk in snorts and hisses with her favorite brother, Chomp.

She snatched at dragonflies,

crunched on crawfish,

and floated on her belly with her eyes barely peeking out of the water.

Sue worked hard to learn Mama Coco's lessons, but it didn't come easy. While her brothers and sisters could steer themselves through the water with their powerful notched tails, Sue's hind end just ended. Her fingers and toes weren't webbed for swimming, and her teeth never did get long and pointy like theirs.

Chomp and the others teased her from sunup to sundown, but Mama Coco would always say, "Y'all leave Sue alone. She is what she is."

During the warm months, Chomp spent his time floating as still as a fallen log till some food came by and presented itself for supper. Sue would do her best to make like a log—until a whiny mosquito bit into her bony, sunburnt shoulder.

"Be still," Chomp would hiss, "or else we'll never catch nothin'."

Sue tried her best. But she couldn't help noticing that Chomp didn't have any ears for a mosquito to whine in. And his skin was so thick that no piddling little insect ever pestered him.

When winter blew its cold breath through the swamp, Mama Coco, Chomp, and the others tucked themselves into their cozy den to nap and wait for spring. But Sue couldn't sleep that long and would stay awake, shivering and listening to her stomach growl.

Come spring, as the Alligators grew faster than swamp grass, Chomp began to practice his newfound bellow. He'd raise his tail, swell himself up, and let out a *GRON-NK!* that shook the leaves off the trees.

"Let's hear you beat that," said Chomp one warm morning.

Sue pulled in a breath, raised up her fanny, and gave it her best shot. "Wo-o-onk!" The sound was so puny that Chomp and the others nearly drowned themselves laughing.

Red-faced and mad as a fire ant, Sue turned the tail she didn't have and swam away.

PART TWO
GiRL

"Who wants to bellow anyway?" said Sue to herself. She took off on the Gator trails that wound through the marshes, not sure what she was looking for, but sure she had to find it.

At last she rounded a bend in a faraway corner of the swamp.
There, like a half-remembered dream, floated a houseboat.

A voice behind her said, "I always knowed this day would
come." It was Mama Coco.

"What is this place, Mama?" asked Sue.

"Honey chile," said Mama Coco, "this here's the houseboat
where you used to live with your real mama and daddy."

"Aren't *you* my real mama?" asked Sue.

"I'm as real as ever, dahlin'," said Mama Coco, "but I ain't no
Human Being. And you ain't no Alligator. You're a Girl."

"A Girl?" The word echoed in Sue's memory. Mama Coco gave a wise nod, and pointed her snout at Sue's knobby-kneed limbs. "You're meant to stand up on those. Go on now, try it."

"A Girl," whispered Sue. Hoisting herself onto the deck, she stretched out one trembly leg, then the other. Her knees creaked as she stood herself up—and fell right back into the swamp.

Even Mama Coco had to hide a crocodile grin as she helped her back onto the houseboat. "Try again, honey chile."

Dripping with duckweed, Sue staggered to her feet. This time she took a step or two before she tumbled back into the water. But try again she did, and soon found that maybe she was meant to be a two-legged after all.

Sue tugged open the saggy screen door. Inside, it was dusty and musty, but the memory of something good to eat drifted through the cobwebby kitchen. And it seemed a song floated on the air, a song sung in a voice as rich as pecan pralines.

"Where are my mama and daddy?" asked Sue.

"Word in the swamp is they went out to look for you and was blowed away by the Hurricane that brought you to me," said Mama Coco gently. "And now I'll leave you to find out what it's like to be a Girl again."

"All by myself?" Sue gulped.

"You're the onliest one that can do it," said Mama Coco. "Besides, it's time all you children start finding your own dens." And giving Sue an Alligator kiss, Mama Coco turned and swam away.

So, in her newfound old home, Sue tried to settle into being a Girl. With every sunrise, she remembered to remember more of her two-legged ways.

She found a homespun dress of her mama's to wear over her ragtag tatters so the mosquitoes couldn't have her for supper every night. After scorching nine out of her ten fingers, she puzzled out how to work the cookstove, and discovered that everything tasted better with wild rice and hot gravy.

Then Sue unearthed her daddy's old accordion, all covered with cobwebs. When she stretched out its bellows and mashed down on some buttons, it made a gosh-awful noise. But in all that racket she recognized the faint song that had almost faded from the back room of her memory. She even recalled the old words, "*O yé yaie, mon coeur fait mal.*"

It was true—Sue's heart *did* ache. In fact, some days it hurt so bad she thought it would split right down the middle.

She missed Mama Coco, she missed the comforting grunts and hisses of her Alligator family—why, she even missed Chomp's never-ending teasing.

One day, when the wind brought her the sound of an Alligator bellow, she jumped in her daddy's pirogue and paddled to her old stomping grounds. There she found Mama Coco tending a new nestful of eggs.

"What's that long face for, honey chile?" said Mama Coco.

"It's lonesome being a Girl," Sue complained. "How come nobody comes to visit me?"

"Why, they're digging out their dens and practicing their bellows," said Mama Coco. "Busy being Alligators."

"It's not fair," said Sue. "If I'm a Girl, I can't be a Gator. And if I'm a Gator, I can't be a Girl."

"All you can do is be who you is," said Mama Coco.

"But that's just it," said Sue. "Who *am* I?"

PART THREE

ALLIGATOR SUE

Lonesome for her favorite brother, Sue paddled her pirogue in the direction of Chomp's new den. But as she went farther into the swamp, the air began to feel heavier than a catfish's bath towel; it was hot enough to melt the wax in your ears.

She held up a finger and sniffed. Just then a great crash of thunder rumbled through the swamp.

Fierce black clouds swirled over the trees. Sue's knees started knocking. The wind began to wail. Sue's teeth started clacking. She knew this was no ordinary storm—it was a Hurricane!

The clouds opened up and the rain poured down. Up ahead was Chomp's Gator hole. But the wind slammed against the pirogue, driving Sue backward. Any minute now, that Hurricane would reach down and blow her away, just like it had done once before.

In a flash of lightning, Sue remembered the Alligator lessons she'd been taught. Tying her pirogue to a tree, she dove into the murky deep. With stroke after powerful stroke, she soon made it to her brother's Gator hole, far from the gusty fingers of the Hurricane.

Sue found Chomp deep in his new den, cozy as a caterpillar in a cocoon. "Am I glad to see you!" she gasped. "I thought that Hurricane would get me for sure."

"I'm glad you came to visit," said Chomp with a toothy smile. "I ain't had nobody to pick on lately."

Sue grinned at him and tried to catch her breath.

Suddenly she remembered. "Mama Coco!"

"Huh?" said Chomp with a yawn.

"She's guarding her nest—she'll never leave her new eggs. We've got to help her!"

Heaving a deep breath, Sue plunged back into the water, with Chomp close behind. Trees crashed around them, and critters whooshed by on the wind. Sue and Chomp swam with all their might. Sure enough, they found Mama Coco sprawled over her nest, guarding her eggs from the fierce waves that licked closer and closer.

Quicker than quick, Sue grabbed an armful of eggs and tucked them with some Spanish moss into the pirogue. Chomp and Mama Coco joined in, and just as they loaded in the last egg, the water swallowed Mama Coco's nest with one great gulp.

"Hurry, Mama," said Sue, "climb on up." And grabbing on to the pirogue, Sue and Chomp began to pull.

The Hurricane roared, and each flash of lightning showed the swamp rising higher. Dodging whirlpools and floating logs, Sue and Chomp steered the pirogue through the choppy waters. Just as Sue thought she couldn't swim another stroke, they rounded the bend and spotted the houseboat.

Scrambling up on deck, Sue grabbed a big pine basket, and into it the three of them piled every last Gator egg. Then they dragged the basket inside, away from the driving rain.

But still that storm wouldn't give up. It lashed at the windows and pounded the roof. The boat rocked on its moorings like a crazy cradle. Sue was sure that any second the Hurricane would whoosh her, houseboat and all, into the angry sky.

That's when she spotted her daddy's accordion. Maybe she could lick that storm at its own game! She picked up the accordion, stretched open its bellows, and mashed down on a button. WON-NK! A thunderous note rang out.

Outside, the fury of the Hurricane seemed to pause. Pushing another button, Sue squeezed the bellows. ZON-NK! She threw back her head and sang at the top of her rackety voice, "*O yé yaie, mon coeur fait mal!*"

She pushed and pulled on that accordion with all her might, pulling tune after tune from the back room of her memory. She made such a gosh-awful ruckus that the dishes clattered and the windows rattled.

Chomp joined in with a mighty GRON-NK that was soon answered by all the other Gators in the swamp. Before long, the swamp rang with so much racket that the Hurricane had no choice but to back down, turn tail, and go home.

As the sun broke out hotter than a cayenne pepper, Mama Coco heaved a sigh of relief. "Your bellowing saved my babies, Sue," she said, a tear rolling down her leathery cheek.

Sue planted a kiss on her snout. "Like you once saved me."

Just then they heard some tiny grunts coming from the basket of eggs. "My babies are hatching!" cried Mama Coco. And sure enough, the eggs began to bust open, and bulgy-eyed stripedy little Gators began to wriggle out.

"Sue," said Mama Coco, "will you do me the honor of being godmama to this batch of youngsters?"

Sue grinned from here to Kingdom Come. "Why, I'd be honored," she said.

So Chomp towed Sue's houseboat to a spot halfway between his den and Mama Coco's. And Sue got so good at bellowing on her accordion that before long everyone for miles around, both two-leggeds and four-leggeds, started coming by every Saturday night for a *fais do do*.

As they all two-stepped and toe-tapped, Sue would sing out new songs—her songs—at the top of her rackety voice. But now every one of them ended with "*O yé yaie, mon coeur fait plus mal!*", French for "Oh dear, my heart *doesn't* ache anymore."

Because the truth was, her heart had quit hurting. In fact, it felt like it had been put back together.

At last she knew who she was—Suzanne Marie Sabine
Chicot Thibodeaux, half Gator and half Girl . . .

Alligator Sue, that is.